D0016474

J is for Jackpot...

Dink ran his fingers over the striped wallpaper. Just above his head, he felt a thin crack. He followed the crack with his fingers until he felt another crack, this one running down toward the floor.

Dink jumped back as if his hand had been burned. "Guys!" he shouted.

Josh and Ruth Rose came running into James's office.

Dink showed them his discovery. "I think it's a secret door!" he said.

To Alan Mann and Kate Ford, for their support and bed and board.
—*R.R.*

To New York City, for 17 great years.
—*J.S.G.*

Text copyright © 2000 by Ron Roy
Illustrations copyright © 2000 by John Steven Gurney
All rights reserved under International and Pan-American Copyright Conventions.
Published in the United States by Random House, Inc., New York, and
simultaneously in Canada by Random House of Canada Limited, Toronto.

www.randomhouse.com/kids

Library of Congress Cataloging-in-Publication Data
Roy, Ron.
The jaguar's jewel / by Ron Roy ; illustrated by John Steven Gurney.
p.   cm. — (A to Z mysteries)
"A Stepping Stone book."
Summary: Dink and his friends use their detective skills to locate a giant emerald
missing from a statue delivered to Uncle Warren's museum in New York City.
ISBN 0-679-89458-6 (trade) — ISBN 0-679-99458-0 (lib. bdg.)
[1. New York (N.Y.)—Fiction.   2. Mystery and detective stories.]   I. Gurney, John, ill.
II. Title. PZ7.R8139Jac   2000   [Fic]—dc21   99-40056

Printed in the United States of America   February 2000   40 39 38 37 36 35 34 33 32 31 3

A to Z Mysteries

The Jaguar's Jewel

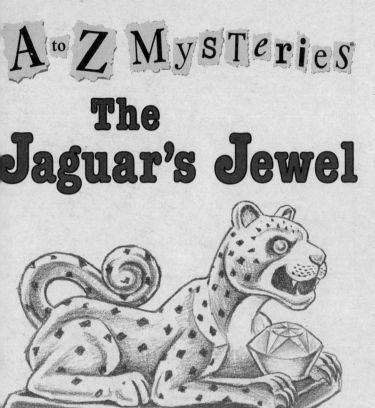

by **Ron Roy**

illustrated by
John Steven Gurney

A STEPPING STONE BOOK™

Random House 🏠 New York

Chapter 1

Dink spread the note on his knees and read it out loud.

Dear Nephew Donny,

I am so happy that you're coming to visit! You and your friends are going to love New York City. I will meet your train at four o'clock on Friday, at Grand Central Station.

Love,
Uncle Warren

1

Josh giggled. "He calls you Donny?"

"Yeah," Dink said, blushing. "But if *you* ever do, I'll tell all the kids at school your middle name is Carol."

"But my middle name *isn't* Carol!" Josh said.

Dink flashed an evil grin. "So?"

"Guys, I think we're there," Ruth Rose said.

The train slowed. Suddenly, the bright, sunny day vanished. Everything outside the train windows turned black.

"Hey, what happened?" Josh cried.

Dink laughed. "We're in a tunnel, Josh," he said. "Don't worry. Ruth Rose and I will protect you."

The train slowed even more, then stopped. "New York, Grand Central Station!" the conductor called. "Last stop! All passengers off!"

The kids grabbed their backpacks

and followed the other passengers to the door.

"Watch your step," the conductor said. He helped the kids hop onto the platform.

They found themselves standing in a concrete tunnel. The dust and soot coming up from under the train made Dink sneeze.

"Where do we go?" Josh asked.

"My uncle said he'd meet us," Dink said. "Maybe we should just wait here."

All around them, people were hurrying along the platform. Dink stood on tiptoe, but he couldn't see his uncle anywhere.

"Is that him?" Ruth Rose asked.

She pointed to a short man in a gray suit. He was pushing toward them through the crowd.

Dink jumped up and down and waved. "Uncle Warren, here we are!"

Uncle Warren Duncan had white hair and a big smile. He carried an umbrella and wore a red carnation in his lapel. His eyeglasses twinkled in the underground lights.

"Donny, welcome!" he said, beaming at the kids. "How was your train ride? Are you hungry?"

"We're fine," Dink said. "The train was great, and Mom packed sandwiches for us."

"Splendid!" Dink's uncle gave him a big hug.

"And whom have we here?" he asked,

peering through his round glasses.

"Josh and Ruth Rose," Dink said, "my best friends!"

"Marvelous!" Uncle Warren said, shaking their hands. "Now let's go find a cab. Follow me!"

Uncle Warren marched up a long ramp with the kids right behind him. A moment later, they entered the biggest room Dink had ever seen.

Hundreds of people bustled in every direction. A deep voice announcing train arrivals and departures echoed over a loudspeaker. Piles of luggage were heaped around the gleaming marble floor.

Try as he might, Dink couldn't take it all in. Uncle Warren said, "This is Grand Central Station's main terminal. Look up!"

The kids tipped their heads back and looked up...and up! Gold-painted stars and animals danced across an emerald green ceiling.

"This is so awesome!" Josh said. "Look, there's a bull and a goat!"

"Taurus and Capricorn—the zodiac signs, dear boy," Uncle Warren explained. "Now onward!"

Uncle Warren marched them toward an exit. The kids followed him out of the building.

The street outside Grand Central Station was a shock to Dink. His ears were blasted by horns honking, brakes

squealing, music blaring, and food ven-
dors shouting.

"Welcome to the Big Apple!" Uncle
Warren said.

He waved his umbrella and whis-
tled. A yellow cab zoomed up and
screeched to a halt inches from Uncle
Warren's shiny black shoes.

Uncle Warren yanked open the rear
door. "In, youngsters, in!" he cried.

They had barely sat down and shut
the door when the cab lurched back
into traffic.

"Where to?" the driver asked over her shoulder.

"Number three forty, West One Hundred and Tenth Street," Uncle Warren said.

He turned to the kids. "We'll stop at the museum first," he said. "I'm expecting a shipment from South America."

Dink sat up as the driver zigzagged her way up a wide avenue. With his nose to the glass, Dink watched thousands of cars, taxis, buses, bikes, and people dodge one another. Even through the closed taxi window, he could feel the throbbing pulse of the huge city.

Twenty minutes later, the cab hurtled to a stop in front of a building made of white marble. "Here we are," the driver said.

Uncle Warren handed her a few bills. "Keep the change, please."

"Thanks, mister!" the driver said, smiling into her rearview mirror.

Uncle Warren and the kids piled out of the taxi.

"This is where I work," Uncle Warren said. He pointed to a small brass sign next to a green door. The sign read THE PORTER MUSEUM.

Dink noticed that it was a lot quieter here. Trees stood in front of the buildings, and a few kids were drawing chalk pictures on the sidewalk. From a window across the street came the sound of someone playing a piano.

Suddenly, he heard a voice call out, "Warren! Hello!"

Dink saw a smiling man and woman standing in front of a small restaurant next to the museum.

Behind them, a sign above a wide window read LE PETIT BISTRO.

"Come meet my friends," Uncle

Warren said, heading toward the couple.

He introduced the kids. "And this is Jean-Paul and his wife, Yvonne," Uncle Warren said.

Uncle Warren pointed to the sign. "These lovely people own the best French restaurant in New York!"

"Hello," the man and woman said, smiling.

"Nice to meet you," the kids said all together.

Yvonne turned to Uncle Warren. "It came!" she said. "A big, heavy box. Four men carried it upstairs to your office."

Jean-Paul reached into his pocket. "I went up with them, then locked the door when they left," he said, dropping a key on a brass ring into Uncle Warren's hand.

"What's in the box?" Dink asked.

Uncle Warren winked. "Nothing much," he said. "Only priceless gold!"

Chapter 2

The kids followed Uncle Warren through the green door. They climbed carpeted stairs to a door with a frosted-glass window. Uncle Warren unlocked it, and they walked into a spacious, dimly lit office.

A wooden crate nearly as tall as Dink sat on the floor.

Dink looked around the room. A desk and some chairs were arranged on an Oriental rug. A fish tank bubbled quietly near the desk. Against one wall stood a bookcase.

Dink peeked through another door and saw a computer on a desk, a file cabinet, and some bookshelves.

"My assistant works in there," Uncle Warren said. "He took the afternoon off. It's his daughter's birthday, and they've gone to the zoo."

"You have a zoo?" Josh asked.

"Yes, right here in Manhattan we have the Central Park Zoo," Uncle Warren said. "It's pretty small, but there's also the Bronx Zoo, which is enormous!"

Uncle Warren flipped up three switches on the wall. Suddenly, a ceiling fan began whirring around. Music came from hidden speakers. Overhead lights beamed down on them.

"This is a cool office!" Dink said.

"Thank you," his uncle said. He

pointed to the fish tank. "Who'd like to feed my little friends?"

"I would!" Ruth Rose said.

Uncle Warren handed her a container of fish food and showed her how much food to sprinkle on the water.

"Look at this!" Josh said, lifting a shiny silver dagger off the desk. The blade was curved, and the handle was shaped like a soaring hawk.

"Careful," Uncle Warren said. "It's sharp! I use it as a letter opener."

"Is it real silver?" Josh asked.

Uncle Warren nodded. "It was made in Spain more than three hundred years ago."

"I can see my reflection in it!" Josh said.

Uncle Warren laughed. "That's because my assistant polishes it every morning."

Josh wiped the letter opener on his T-shirt and placed it back on the desk.

"Now, let's see what we have here," Uncle Warren said. He draped his suit jacket over a chair, then dragged a toolbox from a closet. He selected a small crowbar from among the tools. Fitting the sharp end of the bar under the crate's lid, he pried the top off.

Inside were mounds of white packing "peanuts." Uncle Warren reached through the peanuts and pulled out a small package wrapped in brown paper.

He stripped away the paper to reveal a layer of plastic bubble wrap. He carefully removed the plastic and held up a gold cup.

"Cool!" said Josh.

Uncle Warren grinned at the kids. "Lovely, isn't it?" he said. "This is a drinking cup made by the Incan people in the fifteen hundreds. Imagine, almost five hundred years ago! Have you studied the Incas in school?"

The kids shook their heads.

"Well, the Incas lived in Peru, in South America. The Porter Museum is going to display some of their pottery and gold sculpture."

Leaning over the side of the crate, Uncle Warren dug deeper into the peanuts. "Aha, I think this is the jaguar!"

Grunting, he lifted out a much bigger package. It was as long as Dink's arm and nearly as big around as his waist. The heavy package made a solid

thud as Uncle Warren set it on his desk.

"Why's it so heavy?" Josh asked.

"Gold is a heavy metal," Uncle Warren explained. "The Incas admired jaguars for their strength and cunning. This one is made of solid gold. It holds a fabulous emerald in its front paws."

"Can we see it?" asked Ruth Rose.

"Yes, but not until tomorrow," he said. "A Dr. Pitts will be here at nine o'clock. He works for the Society of Incan Treasures. Dr. Pitts will inspect every piece as it comes out of its wrapping."

"Why?" Josh asked.

"To make sure everything has arrived safely," Uncle Warren said. "These pieces are priceless treasures!"

Uncle Warren put the jaguar back in the crate. "Sleep well!" he said.

Then he reached into the toolbox and handed Josh a hammer. "Let's rewrap the cup and put it back, then nail the crate shut again till tomorrow."

After they'd finished, Uncle Warren said, "Now let's lock up and walk to my apartment. We'll leave your backpacks with Roger, then I'll treat you to a New York dinner!"

"Who's Roger?" Ruth Rose asked.

"He's the doorman at my apartment building," Uncle Warren said. "He opens the door for tenants and whistles for taxis."

"Can we eat at your friends' restaurant?" Josh asked.

"Yes, but not tonight," Uncle Warren said. "I'm saving that for your last night in the city. What kind of food do you like?"

"Pizza and ice cream!" Josh said.

Dink laughed. "Josh will eat anything," he said.

"I mean, do you want Japanese, Chinese, Italian, Greek, Indian, or Mexican food?" Dink's uncle asked.

"Why don't you pick?" Dink said. "We love surprises!"

Uncle Warren flipped down the wall switches. The lights, music, and ceiling fan all went off. The kids followed him out of the office.

"Then a surprise you shall have!" he said, and pulled the door shut behind them.

Chapter 3

Dink's uncle lived in a squat gray building a few blocks from the museum.

A tall man in a green uniform opened the doors.

"Good evening, Mr. Duncan," the man said.

"Hello, Roger. Kids, this is Roger Hobart." Uncle Warren put his hand on Dink's shoulder. "This is my nephew, Donny, and these are his pals from Connecticut, Josh and Ruth Rose."

Roger smiled at the kids. "Welcome to New York," he said.

"Will you watch their backpacks while we're out?" Uncle Warren asked. "I'm taking the kids for dinner. Any suggestions?"

Roger rubbed his stomach. "How about the Panda Palace, for Chinese?"

"Perfect!" Uncle Warren said. "How about it, kids?"

"I've never eaten Chinese food," Josh said. "What's it like?"

"Delicious, and there are about a million choices on the menu," Roger said.

"All right!" Josh said.

"I'm game," Dink said.

"Me too!" Ruth Rose said. "Can we eat with chopsticks?"

Uncle Warren laughed. "Of course!"

They walked to a street called Broadway. The wide sidewalks were crowded with people. Lights began to come on in store windows. A man leaned against a building, playing softly on a saxophone. The saxophone case lay open at his feet.

"Look!" Josh whispered. "There's money in that guy's case!"

"If people like his playing, they give him money," Uncle Warren explained. He dropped a dollar bill into the case. The kids each dropped some change in, getting a smile from the sax player.

"Here we are," Uncle Warren said a few minutes later. The Panda Palace had a shiny red door with fake panda bears standing on either side. A smiling host welcomed them to the restaurant.

Two hours later, Josh leaned back from the table. "I'm stuffed!" he said.

Their waitress brought the bill and placed a fortune cookie in front of each of them.

"Inside these cookies you'll find a slip of paper telling your fortune," Uncle Warren said. "Some people think that if you eat the cookie, your fortune will come true!"

"Can I save mine till later?" Dink

asked. "My stomach is ready to bust!"

"Good idea. We'll have the cookies at home," Uncle Warren said. He paid the bill, and they left the Panda Palace.

"By the way, what were those black slimy things on my chicken?" Josh asked as they walked along Broadway.

"Seaweed," Dink said.

"No way!"

"Donny is right," Uncle Warren said. "But seaweed is good for you!"

"Good for fish, maybe," Josh said.

It started to rain, so they walked quickly. At the apartment, Roger handed them their backpacks. "How was dinner?" he asked.

"I ate black seaweed," Josh muttered.

Roger grinned. "Good stuff, isn't it?" he asked.

Uncle Warren and the kids rode the elevator to the tenth floor, then walked down the hall to a gray door.

"Welcome to my little apartment," Uncle Warren said, and led them inside.

Uncle Warren's living room was filled with old, comfortable-looking furniture. The carpet on the floor was thick and soft. Paintings hung on the white walls between overflowing bookcases.

"Neat place, Uncle Warren," Dink said.

"Thank you, Donny. Ruth Rose, you get the guest room," Uncle Warren said. "You two boys can share the fold-out sofa here in the living room."

When they were all in their pajamas, they gathered around the dining room table to open their fortune cookies.

"The oldest gets to read his first," Uncle Warren said, cracking open his cookie.

He read his fortune silently, then laughed out loud. "Mine already came true. It says that I will meet nice people today, and I have!"

"Me next!" Josh said. He broke open his cookie and pulled out the thin paper. He read out loud: "'Strange foods will please you.'"

Josh made a face. "I already ate seaweed," he said. "I can't wait to see what's next!"

"My turn," Ruth Rose said. She ate her cookie and looked at the fortune inside. "Oh, boy. This says I'll find treasure in unexpected places!"

"Your turn, nephew," Dink's uncle said. "Then it's to bed for all of us. We have a busy day tomorrow."

Dink cracked open his cookie and read his fortune to himself. "I don't get it," he said.

"Out loud, Dink!" Josh said.

Dink read: "'Your eyes will play tricks on you.'"

His uncle smiled. "Right now, your eyes look pretty sleepy, nephew. Off to slumberland!"

After breakfast the next morning, Uncle Warren and the kids walked back to the museum. It was still raining, so they huddled under two umbrellas.

They left the dripping umbrellas on the small landing at the top of the stairs. Another wet umbrella already stood in the umbrella stand. Uncle Warren opened the door, and they walked into his office.

A man greeted them just inside the door.

"Ah, James, you're here," Dink's uncle said. "Kids, this is James Pride, my assistant. James, this is my nephew, Donny Duncan, and his friends, Josh and Ruth Rose."

James Pride smiled at the kids. "Has

Warren taken you sightseeing?" he asked.

"Not yet," Uncle Warren said. "But I've promised them a buggy ride through Central Park when the rain stops!"

James tapped the wooden crate. "I'll leave this to you, Warren," he said. "My daughter loved the zoo, but now I'm behind on paperwork." He walked into his office and closed the door.

Just then, there was a knock on the outer office door. Uncle Warren opened it to a man in a wet raincoat.

"I'm Dr. Jeremy Pitts," the man said. "I believe Mr. Duncan is expecting me."

"Indeed I am, Dr. Pitts!" Dink's uncle said. He shook the man's hand. "Come in and dry off. Care for some tea?"

"No, thank you, I had breakfast at my hotel," Dr. Pitts said. He glanced around the office, then walked over to the large crate. "I see the treasures have arrived."

"Yes, the box came yesterday," Dink's uncle said. "Hang up your wet things and we'll get to work."

Once more, Uncle Warren pried off the crate's lid. He lifted each piece from the crate and handed it to Dr. Pitts, who carefully removed the wrappings. Using a special magnifying glass, he examined each item, then checked it off a list.

The kids helped by re-wrapping the treasures. There were several more gold cups, a few carved animals, some pottery, and colorful masks made of jade and feathers.

"This all looks in fine condition," Dr. Pitts said. He glanced at his list. "But where is the jaguar, Mr. Duncan?"

Dink's uncle reached down into the crate. "Donny, can you give me a hand?" he asked.

Dink hurried over, and together

they lifted the long, heavy package out of the crate.

"Place it here, please," Dr. Pitts said. He stood near the right side of Uncle Warren's desk.

"Watch the fish tank, Donny," Dink's uncle said as they set the heavy package down on the desk.

They all gathered around as Dr. Pitts stripped away the brown paper.

Josh let out a gasp as the plastic bubble wrap was removed.

The jaguar was solid gold. It was lying down, staring out of ruby eyes. Between its front paws was an emerald the size of a golf ball. The green jewel blazed under the office lights.

"Isn't it spectacular, kids?" Uncle Warren asked. "What workmanship!"

Dr. Pitts wiped his hands on a handkerchief. Then he stroked the golden cat, feeling each curve and muscle.

"What's this?" he said suddenly, bending over the jewel.

"Something wrong?" Dink's uncle said.

Dr. Pitts peered through his magnifying glass at the jewel.

A minute later, he raised his head and looked at Dink's uncle. "Sir, this stone is a fake!"

Chapter 4

"What do you mean?" Dink's uncle asked. "I don't see how it could be fake."

Dr. Pitts rested a finger on the jewel. "This is not the original emerald," he explained. "In fact, it is not an emerald at all."

"But how could that be?" Dink's uncle cried.

"Look. I will show you," Dr. Pitts said. He took a small flashlight from his pocket.

"Will you please pull the shades and turn off the lights?" he asked.

Dink was closest to the windows, so he pulled the shades down and clicked off the light over the fish tank. Josh hurried over to the switches on the wall.

When the room was dark, Dr. Pitts turned on his flashlight and shone the beam on the jewel.

Suddenly, the flashlight went out. Dink heard something hit the desktop, then roll off and make a soft thud on the carpet.

"Sorry," Dr. Pitts muttered. "I seem to have dropped my flashlight. Can someone please..."

"I'll get it!" Josh said in the dark. He knelt down and fumbled around under the desk. "Found it," he said a moment later. He stood, switched it on, and aimed the light at the desk.

"Thank you, young man," Dr. Pitts said. He took the flashlight and pointed it at the jewel once more.

"You see, if this were a real emerald, the light would penetrate," he explained. "The light beam would go to the heart of the jewel."

He tapped a finger against the jewel. "But this is just glass. Notice how the light bounces off the surface. The light does not enter the stone."

He shone the light on his own face.

"Of course, that is just my opinion. You are welcome to get another, Mr. Duncan."

"I certainly will!" Dink's uncle said.

He walked over to the wall and switched on the lights.

Dink blinked at the sudden brightness. His uncle looked very upset.

"But I simply can't understand how the real emerald could have been switched for a fake one!" Dink's uncle continued. "Are you absolutely sure?"

Dr. Pitts nodded. "Unfortunately, yes. I am sure."

"Then the swap must have taken place before the crate arrived," Uncle Warren declared. "Perhaps it happened in South America, when the jaguar was wrapped."

Dr. Pitts shook his head. "I'm sorry, but I was there for the packing. I assure you, when the jaguar was put into this crate, the emerald was real."

Dink's uncle stared at the jaguar. "I just don't see how it was possible!" he repeated.

Dr. Pitts shrugged. "Of course, I will have to report this to the police," he said. "If you want that second opinion..."

Dink's uncle hurried across the room and opened the door to James

Pride's office. "James, please call Empire Jewelry on Broadway. Ask Regina Wu to come immediately. Tell her it's urgent!"

While they waited, Dr. Pitts examined the lock on the office door, then wrote something on a small pad.

Uncle Warren slumped in his chair and stared at the statue.

The kids sat on the rug and waited. Dink wanted to say something to his uncle, but he looked too upset.

Long minutes passed, then a knock sounded at the door. Uncle Warren jumped up. He let in a tall woman wearing a black raincoat. "Warren, I came as fast as I could," she said. "The streets are a mess!"

They shook hands, and Dink's uncle explained about the jaguar's jewel. "Dr. Pitts claims it's a fake!"

"May I?" Using a jeweler's magnifying glass, Ms. Wu examined the stone for a few minutes.

Then she removed a small bottle from her pocket and squeezed a drop of liquid onto the jewel. When the liquid dried, she wiped the stone with a cloth.

She shook her head. "He's right," she said. "This is a glass replica."

Uncle Warren fell back into his chair. "I am simply dumbfounded! Where did the switch take place? How? Who could possibly..."

"Pardon me," Dr. Pitts said. "The lock on the door does not appear to have been forced. Who besides you has a key to this office?"

"Mr. James Pride, my assistant, for one," Dink's uncle said. "And my friend Jean-Paul. He owns the restaurant next door to the museum. He let the delivery-men into my office yesterday."

"So this Jean-Paul has a key?" Dr. Pitts asked.

Uncle Warren shook his head. "Not to keep. I lent him my key, since the crate was due while James and I were away from the museum."

"So two people besides yourself had access to the jaguar, is that right?" Dr. Pitts asked. "Your assistant and your friend?"

"That is correct, but I assure you, neither of them has touched that statue. The idea is absurd!"

"Um, excuse me, Uncle Warren?" Dink said.

Everyone turned to look at Dink.

"Wouldn't there be fingerprints? I mean, if someone did take the real jewel, they'd leave prints on the fake one, right?"

No one spoke for a minute. Then Dr. Pitts smiled at Dink. "That's an excellent idea," he said. "And I think we should ask the police to look for fingerprints. They will, of course, find mine.

But unless I miss my guess, no others."

"Why do you say that?" Ruth Rose asked.

"Because, young lady," Dr. Pitts said, "this thief was very clever. And clever thieves wear gloves."

Uncle Warren nodded at the phone. "Please call the police," he told Dr. Pitts. "They will prove that Jean-Paul and James are innocent!"

Dr. Pitts looked at Dink's uncle. "Excuse me, sir, but there is another suspect."

"And who would that be?" Uncle Warren asked.

"Yourself," Dr. Pitts said quietly.

Chapter 5

Dink heard thumping footsteps on the stairs just before two police officers entered the office. They listened to the story, then "invited" Dink's uncle down to the police station to answer more questions.

"Mr. Duncan, will you ask Mr. Pride and Jean-Paul to come with us?" one of the officers asked.

"I will," Dink's uncle said. "But believe me, this is a horrible mistake!"

The officer nodded, pointing to the statue. "We'll have to take this, too. We'll check it for prints at the station."

"What about us?" Regina Wu asked. "Are Dr. Pitts and I free to go?"

"I have your addresses," the officer said. "We know where to find you."

"Of course," Dr. Pitts said. He and Regina Wu left.

Uncle Warren walked over to Dink. "Don't worry, nephew, this shouldn't take long," he said. "Stay with Yvonne until I get back."

When he bent down to hug Dink, he whispered, "Donny, remember your cookie!"

James Pride locked the office, and they all walked down the stairs. The two officers carried the re-wrapped jaguar.

Jean-Paul hugged Yvonne, then joined Uncle Warren and James Pride in one of the police cruisers.

Dink, Josh, Ruth Rose, and Yvonne watched them drive away in the rain.

"Come inside," Yvonne said. "I will make something warm to drink. The men will be back in a jiffy, yes?"

She fixed the kids big mugs of hot chocolate. They sat at the window and watched the rain fall.

"Try not to worry," Yvonne said. "When the men return, then we solve the mystery, yes?"

She left the kids and passed through a blue curtain into the restaurant's kitchen.

"This is so weird!" Josh said.

"It stinks," Dink said. "I know my uncle wouldn't steal some dumb jewel!"

"But what happened to it?" Ruth Rose said. "*Someone* stole the real one!"

The kids sipped their hot chocolate

and looked through the rain-streaked glass.

Dink stood up. "I wonder where the bathroom is?"

"Ask Yvonne," Ruth Rose said. "I think she's in the kitchen."

Josh slurped up the last of his drink. "And see if she has any more hot chocolate!" he said.

Dink walked toward the back of the restaurant. He passed through the blue curtain into the kitchen.

A pile of chopped broccoli sat on the counter next to a bowl of peeled raw onions. He looked around, but Yvonne wasn't there.

He saw another blue curtain, so he peeked through it, looking for the bathroom.

Just then, he heard a noise. Dink turned around and saw Yvonne slip through a narrow door. When the door closed behind her, it disappeared!

Dink blinked his eyes. The door was gone! There was no frame, no knob, and no hinges. He shook his head. Was he seeing things?

Dink found the bathroom, used it, then hurried back to Josh and Ruth Rose.

"Guys, listen to this!" Dink told them about Yvonne and the vanishing door. "After she shut the door, it disappeared, honest!"

"Disappearing doors?" Josh scoffed.

"Maybe it's her private bathroom or something," Ruth Rose said.

Suddenly, Dink remembered what his uncle had said to him. "When my uncle hugged me upstairs, he whispered, 'Remember your cookie' in my ear."

Josh grinned. "Maybe he was hungry," he said.

"Or maybe he was telling you to remember the fortune *in* your cookie!" Ruth Rose said.

"I saved it!" Dink said. He reached into his jacket pocket.

"What...?" Dink pulled out his uncle's brass key ring. "Where'd this come from?"

"That looks like the key to your uncle's office," Josh said.

"You're right!" Dink said. "He must have dropped it into my pocket when he hugged me!"

Dink reached back into his pocket and pulled out the slip of paper from his fortune cookie.

"'Your eyes will play tricks on you,'" he read.

"Your fortune is already coming true!" Ruth Rose said. "I wonder if mine will. I'm supposed to find a treasure."

"Look!" said Josh suddenly. He pointed out the window. "There's that jewelry lady!"

Regina Wu hurried past the restaurant. The kids watched her slip inside the green door that led up to Uncle Warren's office.

"Why is she going back up there?" Dink asked.

Just then, Yvonne came through the blue curtain. She was carrying a pitcher and a plate of cookies.

"More hot chocolate?" she asked. "And some of my special cranberry cookies!"

While Josh and Ruth Rose reached for the cookies, Dink stared out the window at the green door.

Suddenly, the door opened, and Regina Wu stepped back outside. She closed the door behind her, then hurried away from the building.

Dink watched her dash up the street, raising her umbrella.

He stared after Regina Wu. *What's going on?* he wondered. *Why would she go up to the office when she knows my uncle isn't there?*

Suddenly, another thought struck him. *Unless she went up to the office* because *he isn't there!*

Chapter 6

Dink waited until Yvonne went back to the kitchen, then told the others what he'd just seen.

"But the office is locked," Josh said.

"Maybe she has a key," said Dink.

"Where would she get a key?" Josh asked. "You have one, and James Pride has the other."

"The question is," Ruth Rose said, "why did she go up there now, when nobody's around?"

Dink stood up. "We need to find out," he said. "Maybe she left a clue! Let's go before Yvonne gets back."

The kids hurried out into the rain. They scooted next door and slipped through the green door.

"Look," Dink said, pointing at the carpet. "Wet footprints!"

They hurried up the stairs. At the top, they saw more wet spots.

Dink's hand was shaking so badly he could barely unlock the door. The office was dark except for the light over the fish tank. The only sound was the tank's bubbling filter.

"This place is creepy," Josh whispered.

Dink checked the floor. "No wet footprints in here," he said quietly.

"Maybe Regina Wu wiped her feet before she came in," Ruth Rose whispered back.

"Maybe," Josh said. "But why are

we whispering?" He flipped up the wall switches, and the lights, ceiling fan, and music all came on.

Dink squinted in the sudden brightness. "Okay," he said, "let's look around."

"For what?" Josh asked.

"I'm not sure," Dink answered. "But Regina Wu came up here for some reason. Either she took something or she left something behind."

"I'll go through the stuff in the crate," Ruth Rose said. "Dink, why don't you check out James's office? Josh, you take the trash can."

"Why do I have to go poking through the trash?" Josh asked.

"Because you're a good detective, and good detectives *always* check the trash," Ruth Rose said.

"Cool!" Josh said. He headed for the trash can next to the desk.

Dink walked into Mr. Pride's office.

There was a small desk with locked drawers. A framed picture of three people stood on the desk. Dink recognized James Pride. The woman and child must be his wife and daughter, he thought.

Dink checked a gray file cabinet in one corner. It was locked. Then he ran his fingers across the bookshelves. He checked inside some of the books, not knowing what he was looking for. He even peeked under the rug. He couldn't

tell if anything was missing, and he found no clues.

As he started to leave, Dink suddenly noticed that one wall seemed different from the others. He stared at it, trying to figure out what looked odd about it.

Then he realized what it was: this wall had no bookshelves, no file cabinets, no pictures, no anything! It was completely bare.

Dink stepped closer and ran his fingers over the striped wallpaper. Just above his head, he felt a thin crack. He followed the crack with his fingers until he felt another crack, this one running down toward the floor. Two feet in the opposite direction, a third crack ran to the floor. The cracks were almost hidden in the wallpaper.

Dink jumped back as if his hand had been burned. "Guys!" he shouted.

Josh and Ruth Rose came running into James's office.

Dink showed them his discovery. "I think it's a secret door!" he said.

He tried to force his fingers into the cracks, but the door wouldn't budge.

"If there were stairs behind this wall," Ruth Rose said, "they would lead right to the secret door in Yvonne's kitchen!"

Josh's eyes opened wide. "That

would mean she could get in here without a key!"

"Do you think she was coming here when I saw her downstairs?" Dink asked.

"Maybe she met Regina Wu!" Ruth Rose said. "Yvonne could have let her in."

"Maybe," Dink said, walking back to his uncle's office. "But why? We gotta keep looking. Did you find anything in the trash, Josh?"

"Zilch," Josh said.

On the floor where Ruth Rose had been sitting was a pile of packing peanuts. She had unwrapped each artifact, then put it aside.

"All I found was the same treasures we looked at yesterday," she said. "I don't think anything is missing."

The kids continued to search. Behind curtains. Under the Oriental rug. They pulled out everything from every desk drawer. They even dug in the dirt in the potted plants next to the windows.

"Nothing but a secret door that doesn't open," Josh muttered.

"And we can't check out the door downstairs with Yvonne in the kitchen," Ruth Rose said.

"So now what?" Josh asked.

"I don't know," Dink said. He looked at Josh and Ruth Rose. "But my uncle is counting on us to find something up here, and I'm not gonna stop till I find it!"

Chapter 7

"But we've already looked at everything," Josh said, flopping down on the rug.

Ruth Rose walked over to the fish tank and picked up the container of food.

"That's weird," she said. "There are already some flakes floating on the water. Did one of you guys feed the fish?"

"I didn't," Dink said.

"Me neither," said Josh.

Ruth Rose looked at the food float-ing on the top. "Well, someone did."

"Maybe it was the fish fairy," Josh said.

"OH MY GOSH!" Ruth Rose screamed.

"What's the matter?" Dink asked. Josh jumped to his feet, and he and Dink hurried over.

"Look what's on the bottom!" Ruth Rose said. She pointed down through the water.

Josh put his nose up against the glass. "Looks like a bunch of rocks to me," he said.

Ruth Rose frowned. "Somebody go turn out the lights," she said.

Josh gave Dink a push. "Go ahead, Dinkus!"

Dink hurried over to the wall and flipped down the switches. The music, fan, and lights all went off.

Ruth Rose pointed at the bottom of the tank. "See that glowy green rock? I think it's the jewel!"

Dink elbowed Josh aside and looked at the stone. "No, it's too big," he said. "The emerald was like a golf ball, remember?"

"Things always look bigger underwater," Ruth Rose said. "Your eyes are playing tricks on you again, Dink!"

Ruth Rose reached down and plucked the green rock out of the tank. Water dripped onto the floor as she wiped it on her jeans.

Out of the water, the rock didn't look anything like the other rocks in the fish tank. In the tank light, the rock shone a lustrous green.

"Wow!" Dink said. "It's beautiful!"

"How did it get in there?" Josh asked.

"I guess the thief dumped it in," Dink answered.

"But why would the thief do that?" Josh asked.

Ruth Rose shook her head. "Maybe he needed a quick place to hide it."

Dink nodded. "James *was* here early this morning. Maybe we caught him in the act!"

"I'm turning on the lights," Josh

said. He headed for the wall switches.

"Stop!" Dink said suddenly. "What's that sound?"

"What sound?" Josh asked as he turned on the fan, music, and lights.

Dink walked over and flipped the switches down again. "Now listen," he whispered in the darkness. "Hear it?"

"I think I do," Ruth Rose said. "Like a little buzzing."

"Maybe it's the fish tank," Josh said.

Ruth Rose clicked off the bubbler. "Nope, I still hear it," she said.

"Now I hear it, too," Josh said. "What can it be? Everything's turned off!"

"I'm going to turn on just the lights," Dink said.

When they could see, the kids began prowling around the office.

Dink stopped in front of the bookcase. "Guys, it's louder over here!"

Josh giggled. *"The Case of the Buzzing Books!"* he said.

Dink stood on tiptoe and ran his hands over the shelves. He felt a small button and pushed it. Suddenly, a shelf slid open. "Look!" he cried.

"Hey! Those books are fake!" Josh said. "It's a hidden compartment!"

The space behind the fake books held a small TV set and VCR. With the compartment open, the buzzing was louder. Then the VCR clicked, and the noise stopped.

"It was rewinding," Josh said. "It must have come to the end of the tape. My dad's machine does the same thing."

"Yeah, but rewinding *what?*" Dink asked.

Then the VCR clicked again. The kids watched as a red light came on and the numbers on the machine's face started counting up—:01, :02, :03...

"Hey!" Josh said. "Now it's recording!"

"Maybe your uncle has it for security," Ruth Rose said.

"You could be right, Ruth Rose," Dink said. He glanced at the ceiling. "There must be a camera somewhere in the office."

"Do you think we're on a video?" Ruth Rose said. "Let's take a peek!"

"Good idea!" said Josh.

Dink quickly rewound the tape to the beginning, then turned on the TV and hit "play" on the VCR.

An image came on the screen. For a moment, the tape showed them standing in front of the TV and VCR.

"Cool!" Josh said.

Then the picture jumped and changed. Now the office looked empty and dark. They watched as the office door opened and James Pride walked in.

"This must be earlier today," Ruth Rose said. "James got here before us."

"Maybe it recorded him stealing the jewel!" Josh said.

They watched James walk over and switch on the lights. Then he took off his raincoat and walked into his own office.

The kids looked at each other. James hadn't gone anywhere near the crate.

"Hit 'fast forward,'" Josh said. "We can scan ahead."

Dink pushed the button, and the tape began whirring fast. The picture on the screen flickered.

"Look!" Ruth Rose said. "Something's happening!"

Dink quickly pressed "play." The tape slowed, and the kids saw themselves and Uncle Warren walk into the office.

They watched as they met James

Pride. Then Uncle Warren let in Dr. Pitts. The crate was opened again, and Dr. Pitts checked the contents of each package.

"Now we take the jaguar out of the crate," Dink said.

"And the doc tells us it's a fake," Josh added.

Ruth Rose pointed at the screen. "And here he takes out his flashlight."

"And Dink and I pull the shades and shut off the lights," Josh said.

The picture went black.

The next thing they saw was the light from Dr. Pitts's flashlight. Then it went out.

"This is when you found the flashlight for him," Ruth Rose told Josh.

A minute later, Dr. Pitts had the light in his hand again and was shining it on the jaguar's jewel.

Then the lights came back on. Regina Wu soon showed up, and then the police came. The tape showed everyone leaving the office.

Dink reached out to hit the "stop" button.

"Wait!" Ruth Rose said. "What about Yvonne and Regina Wu?"

"Oh, yeah," said Dink. "Good thinking, Ruth Rose."

They watched the empty office for a while. Dink was about to scan ahead when the door to James Pride's office opened and Yvonne walked in!

"The secret door *does* connect to Yvonne's kitchen!" Ruth Rose said.

They watched as Yvonne walked across the office—straight toward the fish tank! When she got there, Yvonne made kissing noises at the fish. Then she picked up the fish food, sprinkled some into the tank, and turned around and left.

The kids looked at each other. "I guess she's not the thief," said Josh.

Ruth Rose turned back to the TV. "What about Regina Wu?" she asked.

They watched the tape for a few more minutes, but Regina Wu never appeared. Eventually, they saw themselves come through the office door.

Dink stopped the tape and hit the "rewind" button.

"I wonder why your uncle didn't tell the police about this tape?" Josh said. "If they watched it, they'd at least know that James and Yvonne didn't steal the jewel."

Dink nodded. "Yvonne didn't know the jewel was in the fish tank," he said, "so I'll bet Jean-Paul didn't put it there."

Dink looked sad. "And if Regina Wu couldn't even get in the office..."

Ruth Rose let out a gasp. "That means—"

"That means my uncle is the only other suspect," Dink said.

Chapter 8

Josh's mouth fell open. "Your uncle's the thief?" he asked.

"Josh!" Ruth Rose scolded. She turned to Dink. "Your uncle isn't the thief," she said. "He never had a chance to take the jewel. We were with him when he opened the crate, and he sure didn't take it on the tape we just saw."

Dink felt sick even thinking that his uncle might have stolen the emerald. "What about when we turned out all the lights?" he asked.

"But that was so quick," Ruth Rose said. "I don't see how he—"

"Guys! The desk!" Josh said suddenly. "Look at it! Do you see anything different?"

Dink and Ruth Rose looked at Uncle Warren's desk.

"What do you mean?" Dink asked. "There's nothing but the blotter and the letter opener, the same as yesterday and this morning."

Josh hit the "play" button on the VCR. He fast-forwarded until the tape showed the room and everyone in it.

"There!" he shouted a moment later. "Look at the letter opener. The tip is pointing toward the windows, right?"

"Yeah, so what?" Dink said.

"Wait a sec and you'll see."

In the film, the lights went out. After Dr. Pitts finished shining his flashlight on the jewel, the lights came back on.

"Now look!" Josh cried. "See, the letter opener is pointing *away* from the windows. It got turned around!"

"Why does it matter, Josh?" Ruth Rose asked.

"I don't know," Josh said. "But someone picked up the letter opener while the lights were out, then put it down again."

"Who was standing closest to it?" Dink asked, hitting "stop" and "rewind."

"I think Dr. Pitts was," Josh said. "He was standing right in front of the jaguar. The letter opener was a few inches away."

"But why would he want the letter opener in the dark?" Ruth Rose asked.

Just then, they heard thumps outside the office door, like someone stomping on a carpet.

"Who's that?" Ruth Rose whispered.

Josh gulped. "Is the door locked?"

"I don't think so!" Dink whispered back. He swept a hand over the wall switches. The room darkened except for the small light over the fish tank.

"Look!" Josh whispered. Through

the frosted-glass window in the door, the kids saw a tall shadow.

They heard a click, and the door-knob turned.

"Hide!" Dink whispered. "James's office!"

The kids dashed into the small office. Dink left the door open a crack so he could see who entered.

It was Dr. Pitts.

Chapter 9

Dr. Pitts stepped into the dark office. The kids watched him creep toward Uncle Warren's desk.

Suddenly, he switched on his flashlight. Turning slowly, Dr. Pitts played the beam around the room.

In James's office, Dink shrank back against the wall. He held his breath. Next to him, he could feel Josh and Ruth Rose trembling.

Dink dared to peek out again. The flashlight was now lying on the desk. Its beam made a yellow circle on the fish tank.

Dr. Pitts was crouched down, staring into the tank.

Suddenly, he swore. Dink watched Dr. Pitts grab his flashlight and shine it wildly around the room.

Dink froze and held his breath. When he peeked out again, Dr. Pitts was shining the flashlight beam at the floor, near his feet.

He bent over and touched something on the floor.

Dink thought about the water Ruth Rose had dripped there.

Dr. Pitts once more shone the flashlight's beam around the dark office. The light fell on James's door.

"Who's in there?" Dr. Pitts said.

Dink closed his eyes. He felt his

whole body grow cold. Ruth Rose let out a soft gasp.

Then Dink heard footsteps. Dr. Pitts was coming toward their hiding spot!

We have to get out of here! Dink thought. He pressed himself against the wall—but suddenly the wall wasn't there!

Dink felt a strong hand grab his arm. Another hand went over his mouth. Struggling, Dink felt himself being dragged backward.

"Don't speak!" a hoarse voice whispered in his ear. "Come with me!"

Too frightened to resist, Dink let himself be led. He reached out for Josh and Ruth Rose but felt nothing. *Where were they?*

"Down here, quickly!" the voice said.

Dink felt stairs under his feet. As he stumbled down, he smelled something familiar.

At the bottom of the stairs, a door opened. Dink saw light. He smelled onions.

He was in Yvonne's kitchen!

Then Josh and Ruth Rose piled into him. Yvonne released his arm and slammed the door shut. This was the same narrow door Dink had seen her close before.

"Come," Yvonne said, putting a finger to her lips.

Yvonne rushed them toward the front of the restaurant.

"The thief is still up there," she said. "I must lock the outside door. He will be trapped, no?"

She hurried toward the exit, but Dr. Pitts was already racing past the restaurant's window.

"He is gone!" Yvonne wailed. "Now we will never catch him!"

"It's okay," Dink said, grinning. "I

have a feeling we caught him on video."

"Video?" Yvonne asked. "I do not understand."

"My uncle has a hidden camera in the office," Dink explained.

He looked at Josh and Ruth Rose. "I hit the 'rewind' button before we had to hide, remember? I'll bet the tape rewound to the beginning and started recording again before Dr. Pitts came in."

"Not only that," Josh said. "His fingerprints should be on the letter opener!"

"Letter opener?" Yvonne asked, looking at the three kids.

"I think I've figured that out," Ruth Rose said. "When the lights were turned off, he must have used the letter opener to pry the jewel out of the jaguar's paws. Then he quickly switched in the fake and slipped the real jewel into the fish tank."

"But what does it matter, this camera and these fingerprints," Yvonne said, "if he has the jewel?"

"But he doesn't!" Ruth Rose said. She opened her fist and showed the emerald to Yvonne.

"It was in the fish tank, and I got it out before he did!"

"How lovely!" Yvonne said, giving Ruth Rose a hug.

"Now what?" Josh asked.

Yvonne went for the wall phone. "Now we call the police!" she said.

Chapter 10

Jean-Paul held up his water glass. "I propose a toast," he said.

Uncle Warren and Yvonne raised their glasses.

"To three brave and smart kids!" Jean-Paul said, looking at Dink, Josh, and Ruth Rose.

"Hear, hear," Uncle Warren said. "You put a crook behind bars and saved a priceless jewel from being stolen."

"It all started with your telling me to

remember my cookie," Dink told his uncle.

Dink's uncle smiled. "I knew if I gave you my key and reminded you not to trust what you saw, you'd figure it out."

"Ruth Rose's cookie said she'd find a treasure in an unexpected place," Josh said, "and she did!"

"And Josh noticed that the letter opener had been moved," Ruth Rose said.

"Yeah, and Dink found the video recorder behind the books," Josh said.

Dink smiled at Yvonne. "And thank goodness you rescued us!"

"When I came to give you more cookies, you were gone," Yvonne said.

"Then I saw that doctor man sneaking into the downstairs door. I ran up the back stairs!"

"Why do you have those hidden doors?" Ruth Rose asked Dink's uncle.

"Many years ago, the Porter Museum was a private home," he explained. "Old Mr. and Mrs. Porter's servants used that back stairway to go up and down. When the Porter home became a museum, the architects decided to leave the doors and stairway as they were."

"I'm glad they did!" Josh said.

"When I'm away, Yvonne comes up to feed my fish," Uncle Warren said.

Yvonne smiled. "And you thought perhaps I was the one who took the jewel, no?"

Dink blushed. "Yeah, but then I saw Regina Wu sneak into the building, so I thought it was her, too!"

Uncle Warren laughed. "She called a while ago and explained that," he said. "She'd forgotten her umbrella and went back up to get it."

"Uncle Warren," Dink said, "why didn't you tell the police about the camera and the video?"

His uncle laughed. "I honestly forgot the camera was there!" he said. "Besides, I'm a dunce when it comes to anything electronic. James had it installed, but even he tends to forget about it."

"The part I don't understand is how Dr. Pitts could switch the glass emerald for the jewel so fast," Josh said. "And in the dark!"

"I'm sure he practiced," Uncle Warren said. "And when he first came in, he must have spotted the letter opener on my desk."

"So that's why he wanted us to put the jaguar down on the desk close to the fish tank," Dink said. "He knew he was going to slip the emerald into the water."

His uncle nodded. "Yes, and then come back later to get it."

"So when he told you to get a second opinion," Ruth Rose said, "the jewel really *was* a fake. Because he'd just taken the real one, right?"

"Right," Uncle Warren said. "And he almost got away with his scam."

He smiled at his dinner companions. "But he didn't figure on three detectives hiding in James's office!"

Just then, they heard bells jingling outside the restaurant.

"Aha, our ride is here!" Uncle Warren said, standing up.

"What ride?" Dink asked. "Can't we walk back to your apartment?"

"We're not going right back, nephew," his uncle said. "Come!"

He led everyone outside, where a large white horse stood waiting. The horse was harnessed to a buggy. All along the harness leather were small lights and bells.

A short man climbed down from the driver's seat. He wore a spiffy gray suit and a black top hat.

"Hello, I'm Alfie," the man said, "and this lovely horse is Prince."

"Climb aboard!" Uncle Warren said.

"Cool!" Josh said, hoisting himself into the buggy. "Where are we going?"

"Who cares?" Ruth Rose said, climbing in next to Josh.

Uncle Warren helped Dink up and then sat next to him.

"We are going to see New York City by night," he said. "I don't want you to go home thinking all we have here is loud traffic and jewel thieves!"

He tapped on the back of the buggy.

"Take us away, Alfie!"

"Au revoir!" cried Yvonne and Jean-Paul from the sidewalk. "See you tomorrow!"

Alfie clicked his tongue at Prince, and the buggy began to move. Slowly, the horse clip-clopped down the street.

Dink sat back and gazed up at the sky. A billion stars blazed down at him. One star was larger than the others, and it looked green, like a jewel.

The green star blinked, then disappeared.

Dink laughed.

"What's funny?" Josh asked.

Dink shook his head. "Nothing," he said. "Just my eyes playing tricks on me again."

Dear Readers,

When I visit schools, one question I'm often asked is, "Where do you get your ideas for your books?"

The truth is, my ideas come from many places: reading, watching TV, talking with friends, daydreaming. I even get some of my ideas while I'm asleep! I dream a lot, and if a dream contains a great idea, I try to remember it and write it down when I wake up.

Readers like you also give me ideas. A girl in Florida suggested that I use a dog in my series, so now Josh has a basset hound. A boy in Maine sent me a list of words beginning with the letter J. From those words, I chose the title of this book, *The Jaguar's Jewel.*

Many writers write about things that interest them. I happen to be fascinated by animals and history. In *The Jaguar's Jewel,* I was able to combine the two. I also set the story in one of my favorite places to visit, New York City. A lot of what I write about the city is true, but other parts are pure fiction!

I hope you'll write me with some of your ideas for future books. Please visit my Web site at www.ronroy.com or send your letters to:

Ron Roy
c/o Random House Children's Books
1745 Broadway, Mail Drop 11-2
New York, NY 10019

Happy reading!

Sincerely,

Ron Roy

Collect clues with Dink, Josh, and Ruth Rose
in their next exciting adventure,

THE KIDNAPPED KING

Dink tried not to panic. Sammi's parents had been kidnapped, and now Sammi himself had vanished!

Dink hurried back to Sammi's bedroom for one more look. He wasn't in the closet. Where else in the room could a kid hide?

"Any luck?" Dink's mother called from downstairs.

"No, I can't find him!" Dink yelled back.

Then he saw the yellow French book. A paper stuck out like a bookmark.

Dink could see his own name written on the paper, so he pulled it out of the book. Under his name, Dink read five neatly printed words: MY FATHER'S ENEMIES ARE HERE.